Acknowledgments

Firstly my thanks go to Ovingdean Hall School for unleashing my creative mind and giving me the encouragement to keep writing stories, and especially a teacher named Mr Moodley, who advised me never to give up on my writing dream in life.

The tutors of my creative writing courses with The Writers' Bureau and Derbyshire County Council, notably Derek M Fox, who helped nurture my writing 'voice' onto the right track of literary standards, in the process allowing me to achieve writing qualifications.

The editing team at WordsRU for adding clarity to my written prose and Supercovers, whose vision enhances readers' experience through the cover design.

Finally, to my parents for their support and belief in my ability as a writer when things got tough on the creative journey, ensuring that I persevered with my creative ideas. It's not easy to become a published writer, especially when you are deaf, but I did it in the end.

Enjoy the book.

GW00801657

CHAPTER ONE

Mike Harley arrived home with another successful night under his belt. He closed the door to his apartment and caught sight of his face in the hallway mirror. He briefly studied his short, swept-back brown hair, thin cheeks and dropped jaw line, punctuated by clear green eyes; he had a striking look, set off by his immaculate dress style of shirt and tie. He allowed himself a smug smile at the events of the evening as he tugged off his tie and unbuttoned his shirt to reveal a fit lean body.

Mike was ready to call it a night and was en route to the bedroom when he caught sight of the dim red flashing light on the telephone answering machine at the end of the hallway. He debated briefly whether to check the message or leave it until the morning, but curiosity lured him to it. He pressed the play button.

'Mike, it's Jonno,' the voice said against a noisy background of music and chat. 'If you are home in time and value your life, get the hell out of there. You've messed up real bad this time. Two guys are coming after you and believe me, it's no joke.'

Mike frowned and hit the save facility on the answering machine. The doorbell rang. Now uneasy, visions of two heavies waiting to pounce on him from behind his front door made him wary. He edged slowly to the door and looked through the peephole to see who was there, a relieved sigh escaping his lips as he recognised his next-door neighbour. He opened the door to the elderly Mr Roberts.

'I'm glad to catch you home, young Harley. This came for you,' said Roberts in a frail voice. He handed over a parcel.

'You could have given it to me tomorrow,' Mike said. 'It's late.'

'Oh, I wanted to warn you, too. Two men called round earlier. Didn't like the look of them, too shifty for my liking. You be careful, you hear me?'

Mike thanked the old man for his trouble and the warning. Mr Roberts was a proud man who always looked out for those around him and didn't ask for charity from anyone, despite his age. He tipped his finger to Mike and left. Mike closed the door.

The news that the two men had already tried to call on him confirmed for Mike that he really did have a problem. He started to button up his shirt and headed off to the bedroom to pack a bag. This called for a temporary leave of absence.

He racked his brain over what the problem could be; maybe Jonno would be able to inform him when he had safely got himself out of harm's way. Picking up a few shaving items from the top of the chest of drawers by the window, Mike caught sight of a car's headlamps nosing down his street. He saw the car pull up outside and sneaked another look as two burly guys emerged from the vehicle next to the streetlight. One of them looked up and caught Mike at the window. The man raised his arm and pointed, his face contorted with menace.

'Shit,' whispered Mike. They were now hurrying toward his building. Guessing that they were the men he had been warned about, he decided it was time to leave. In panic, he dropped the shaving items into the holdall and zipped it up quickly. He snatched up his fleece jacket from the coat stand near the front door, grabbed his keys and was out of the door, closing it quickly behind him as he made a beeline for the lift. On his approach, he could hear the sound of the lift in motion and looked up at the digital board above the doors. It showed the numbers ascending.

Mike realised he'd have to take the stairway to avoid them. He dashed to the door leading to the stairway and opened it. Fear took hold of him as he heard a male voice coming from below. As he peered down the stairway he heard footsteps drawing nearer. Mike wasn't sure now from which direction they would apprehend him, unless the lift's motion was a decoy. Either way, he didn't want to take a chance and retreated from the doorway.

He went to the nearest corner and slid behind it, just as the lift pinged its arrival on his level. He turned his head a little around the corner of his hiding place, to see the two men emerge from the lift. They turned away from him, their brisk footsteps going towards his apartment until they reached his front door. Mike forced himself away quickly to avoid being seen, should they look in his direction. He heard several knocks upon his door. His breathing became a little shallower, with the fear of being caught once the men realised he had flitted. He heard a door open a little distance away.

'Do you know what time of night this is?' said the all-familiar voice of Mr Roberts in an aggrieved manner. Mike looked again around the corner and saw the two go towards Mr Roberts.

'Go back to bed, old man' said one of the men firmly. He had straggly shoulder-length hair and shabby clothes, Mike observed. 'You've no concern in this matter so leave us be,' he continued, being polite with his request.

'Don't you 'old man' me. Where's your respect? I suggest you both clear off and leave Mr Harley in peace or I'll call the police.' His bravery in confronting the two men was in stark contrast to how Mike Harley was feeling right then.

'You want respect? Sure, no problem,' said the straggly man's partner, a bald-headed, chubby-faced guy, who swiftly moved one of his gloved hands to the back of his black leather jacket and pulled it up a bit. Mike gazed in horror as he saw the glint of a blade, resting in a pouch on the belt clip. He wanted to call out and alert Mr Roberts to the danger but he was frozen in fear.

Early Memory

The man pulled the knife from the pouch and, with a thrust, slammed it home into the old man's chest, his screams muffled by the other hand of the assailant, which was covering his mouth. The old man's eyes widened in shock, there was no resistance given, and the blood began to seep rapidly through his white shirt and drip onto the floor. Mike felt the shakes engulf him as he witnessed the quick jerk of the man's head by the killer's powerful arms and the life was gone. The knife was withdrawn from his chest and the body tossed to the floor, where it quietly thudded on the carpeted corridor.

'He had to go. He would only have ID us and besides—dead people get respect at funerals. Just how the old man wanted it,' remarked the bald man calmly to his accomplice. He bent down over the dead body and wiped the blade clean using the old man's trousers as a cloth.

'The stupid fool should have stayed indoors,' the straggly man said. 'Let's get on with the job.' They turned towards Mike's door, forcing Mike to hide his face again. From his hidden corner he heard another small thud and the squeak of a door's hinge. He looked round the corner, his apartment door was open. The men had forced an entry. This time was crucial for his escape.

Mike put on his fleece, slung the holdall over his shoulder and nervously pulled away from the corner, heading straight for the stairway. As he dashed down the flight of stairs he heard the lift's mechanism in action. The men were probably now on their way down. Mike reached the ground floor and darted across the building's foyer. The lift's doors opened.

'Hey, there's our man!' shouted one of the heavies. Mike upped his pace out of the building and sprinted down the street. He didn't want to look back to gauge the distance between them. He heard a car start up, but no sign of their footsteps behind him and guessed that he had a good lead over them, but not for long—up against the might of a car, Mike knew he needed an alternative.

The car roared with venom and soon the beam of its headlights was rapidly closing in on him. Mike switched to the pavement from the street and remembered a nearby alleyway. He managed to beat the car to its entrance and it was now a game of hide and seek on foot.

The garden walls of the houses in the alleyway offered his only refuge from danger. He leapt upwards at a wall, gripped the top of it and hauled himself over in the nick of time, as headlight beams shone down the alley. Mike heard the car grind to a halt and a door open. The footsteps of one man approached. Mike felt his heartbeat pumping harder and shortage of breath from running left him wheezing a little. He clapped a hand over his mouth to ensure that his position wasn't given away. In the distance, sirens were heard.

'Jemison, let's get out of here,' a faint voice called from the end of the alley, breaking the fleeting standoff between predator and prey. 'The cops are coming.'

'Wherever you are, you won't get far. That's a promise.' Jemison's threat reached out to Mike as his footsteps receded. Mike heard a car door close and the squeal of tyres, and the headlights retreated from the alley. Salvation. Whatever the problem was, the stakes had just been raised, with one man dead and two thugs on his trail.

CHAPTER TWO

DCI Peter Scroggins arrived at the murder scene, his craggy face hardened over the years by the demands of the job, his thinning black hair masked by a small fringe at the front of his forehead. He crouched over the dead man's body and viewed the weapon's entry point.

'Any prints found?' he enquired of the forensic technician taking samples from the body. He swung his head sideways; nothing had been found yet. Scroggins rose up and looked to the front door, the framework dented from the forced entry. He entered the home of Mike Harley. More forensic men in their white suits and gloves were dusting the place for evidence. The acting Crime Scene Manager had greeted Scroggins on his arrival and got the investigation underway.

'It seems to be a case of attempted burglary but the intruders were probably disturbed by Mr Ernest Roberts, the neighbour from next door,' the young detective sergeant Atkins read out from his notebook.

'I disagree. A professional job has been done on the victim,' Scroggins remarked to Atkins. 'No burglar would have done that.' The wisdom and experience from twenty-plus years easily ruled out the rookie's speculations. 'What makes you think more than one person is involved?'

'A couple saw two men enter the lift but didn't see their faces, and shortly after that sighting, people reported hearing a car revving off at speed at around 2300 hours. The murder call was received at 2337 hours.'

Scroggins digested the information given to him. 'Anything missing?'

'Everything seems to be in place, with no valuables touched, sir.' Atkins addressed his superior.

'Who's the occupant?'

'The occupant is Mike Harley, a commercial banker with no previous convictions to report, sir. We have already clarified from other residents here that he doesn't drive.'

Scroggins caught sight of the telephone answering machine. 'Have you checked the machine?'

'Yes, sir, no messages found, and the last number was withheld. But the last call came through at around the time of the murder. It may clarify what happened here.'

Scroggins nodded in agreement with the assumption. He looked at his watch. The time read 0022 hours, the reported car has driven well away from the murder scene by now. 'Good work, Atkins. Finish off here and get the findings. Report to me when you return to the station.' He started to walk away and felt a yearning for a cup of coffee; another long night was in store for him.

A series of sharp nudges to his shoulder woke Mike from his sleep. He looked up to see a woman towering over him, in a long black winter coat. She stood back a little.

'I didn't realise my breakfasts were so popular,' she said, giving a cheery smile.

Mike quickly pulled himself up from the doorstep of the *Midnight Oasis* café and was now face to face with her. She was certainly different as he surveyed her features under a dimly lit street light in the early morning chill of another autumn day.

Her shoulder-length hair was straight and raven black, streaked with a smattering of dark blue at the forefront and on the sides. She wore blue lipstick.

'I hitched a lift in from a lorry driver who recommended this place for breakfast,' answered Mike.

The woman's smile glowed at the compliment and a key was withdrawn from her coat pocket. Mike realised that he was blocking the entrance and moved aside to allow her the access to the café's door. She stepped forward and inserted the key into the lock, turned it and pushed the door open. She released the key and entered inside. She switched the café's lights on.

'Come on in. You can freshen up in the restroom.'

'That's very kind of you, thank you.' Mike picked up his holdall and walked into the café. The woman closed the door behind him and locked it. It wasn't yet opening hours.

'The restroom is over there,' she said and pointed it out to him. 'Do you want a mug of tea?' her kind words of hospitability were not lost on Mike.

'If it isn't a problem,' he spoke, aware that she had to get everything ready for the café's new business day.

'Not a problem at all,' she remarked, her coat now taken off. She was wearing a long, red, and velvet, hippy-style dress that reached down almost to her ankles, held in place by a chain belt. Long black boots up to her knee further accentuated the ensemble. She headed off to the counter and left Mike to go to the restroom.

He took a moment to view his surroundings; there was a row of wooden tables on the well-polished oak floor, with chairs on either side. Each table held an assortment of sauces, a salt/pepper set and a napkin holder. The white painted walls with black Tudor beams displayed pictures of countryside settings. It gave the place a cosy feel for all who ventured into it. Mike took himself to the restroom.

He unpacked the shaving items and a towel. He put the plug in the sink and ran the hot water tap, allowing the sink to fill into a mini lake. Mike started to bathe his face in the water with his hands, tingling from the heat that soothed away the chill he felt from being outside in the chilly morning air. He looked up at the slightly steamed mirror to view his appearance. He looked drawn, the events of the night playing on his mind. What exactly had he done to warrant the murder of his elderly neighbour by the two men? He knew that he had to speak with Jonno soon and get clarification. Mike dropped his head back down and splashed water on his face once more.

He returned to the dining area to find the woman sitting at a table. Two mugs of tea had been placed on it, an indication that she wanted to share her company with him for a while. He took his place at the table.

The woman looked at him. 'Was the hot water okay?' she enquired.

'Yes, it was fine, thank you.' Mike answered, picking up his mug.

'So what brings a city guy like you up here?'

The direct question caught him on the hop. The woman had observed him well from his clothes and accent. She sipped from her mug.

'I needed to get away from things for a while. I'm a merchant banker in London.' There was no hesitation in giving his answer.

'How long are you staying for?' Another probing question was fired from the woman. Mike noticed that she spoke in a concise, clear manner. It reminded him of a business strategy he had been taught. To speak directly and save time in revealing details.

'Well, I'm not sure exactly but it could be weeks for all I know. Why do you ask?'

'It's just that I've a spare room upstairs. It isn't much but you're welcome to it. I feel I can trust you.'

With the hospitality shown again, a thought occurred to Mike. 'Oh, so you own this café?' Mike said surprised. It didn't strike him that the hippy-clad woman with the wild hair could be the owner.

'Yes, I'm certainly the owner,' she chuckled with the cheery smile. She had probably answered this question many times before to unsuspecting customers. 'I'm Midnight.' Her hand reached out for an introductory handshake. He shook it.

'I'm Mike Harley and, yes, I'll take the room upstairs.' The two strangers were now acquainted. 'Midnight, that's certainly an unusual name. So what's your surname?' Mike asked curiously.

'There isn't one.' She rose from the table and picked up her mug. 'I'd better get on and get breakfast underway. We'll discuss the payment for the room later.' And she walked away towards the counter. Mike felt disbelief that Midnight didn't have a surname. She was certainly a mysterious woman to him and there was an allure about her that he had not experienced before. He felt a challenge, maybe, judging from her behaviour and dress sense. He wanted to get to know her better, unravel the mystery behind her cool façade. First, however, he had another matter to sort out.

Thump, thump, thump went the forceful bang on the front door, waking Jonno from his sleep with a start.

'Alright, keep your hair on, I'm coming,' he shouted out and dragged his portly frame out of bed. He picked up the dressing gown from the floor and waddled towards the front door. Once he had the gown on and tied, he opened the door. Shock swept across his face.

'Jonno been a bad boy?' Jemison imitated Jonno, who tried to close the door quickly. He recognised the two men from the nightclub but they were too much of a force for him as they pushed their way into his home. The bald-headed man lurched himself at Jonno, the impact pushing them against a hallway cabinet, causing a lamp to clatter and smash into pieces on the floor.

'Beckett, keep him quiet,' Jemison growled as he shut the door. Beckett covered Jonno's mouth with a hand; the other hand, with swift instinct, drew a knife to Jonno's throat. He was dragged into the lounge and pulled down into an armchair. Jonno was shaking with fear. Beckett kept a grip on him.

'Cooperate with us and we'll spare your life. Is that a fair deal?' Jemison calmly said as he addressed Jonno. Jonno nodded his head. 'Good, what I'd like to know is why did you tip off your friend Mike that we were after him after our chat in the club last night? It wasn't your quarrel or place.' He leant over to Jonno's face as he spoke. Beckett released his hand a little from Jonno's mouth, allowing him to speak, but the knife remained in place at the throat. Jemison cupped a hand to his ear for an answer.

'How did you know I called him?' Jonno nervously responded.

Jemison chuckled mischievously. 'Your friend Mike was in such a rush to escape from us that he forgot to erase your message from the answer machine, but we heard it and he was stupid enough to leave his contacts book by the phone.' Jemison drew his hands to his face in mock horror at the statement. Jonno was caught in a pickle.

'The barman warned me about the reputation of you guys afterwards and I felt that Mike doesn't deserve to die for what he's done,' he answered honestly, his life depending on it.

'Who said anything about him being killed? Did the barman say that?' Jemison said calmly, taken by surprise at the assumption. He retreated from Jonno's face and stood up straight. He looked at Beckett. 'A barman pays us respect. Would you believe it?' Together, the two tormentors gave a hearty chuckle at the plaudits loaded on them over their villainous activities. 'I like the guy, whoever he is.'

'The boss will love that.' Beckett said. The mood quickly descended into seriousness again.

'I can see why you rang Mike but the truth is, Jonno boy, we were given orders to bring him in alive.' Jonno wasn't sure whether to believe Jemison. 'Where could we find him?' He demanded and grabbed the lapels of Jonno's gown.

Jonno felt the fear drive deeper. 'I haven't heard from Mike since we finished work yesterday but I thought it might have been him at the door when you came,' he stuttered. His body shook.

'Not good enough, Jonno,' Jemison retorted with a little rage. A blow struck Jonno's face. The force of it caused the knife to nick his throat, and blood seeped. 'The knife will cut deeper if you...' but the words were interrupted by the ringing of the telephone. Beckett and Jemison looked at one another for a moment and then at Jonno. 'Could it be Mike?' Jemison asked.

'I guess so.'

'Beckett, let him go.' The control over Jonno relinquished, the knife was withdrawn. 'No funny business and if it's Mike, find out where he is.' He ushered Jonno toward the telephone. He walked over to the phone, his hand shakily picking up the receiver.

'Hello?' he quivered, trying to control the emotions of his voice.

'Jonno, it's Mike. What's the hell's going on with these two guys visiting me?'

'We need to meet to discuss it.' He was careful of what he said under the watchful eyes of the thugs. 'Where are you?'

'Never mind where I am, it scared the shit out of me when those guys killed Mr Roberts.' Jonno's face lit with a shocked expression at the news of a death. Jemison saw this and relieved Jonno of the receiver and pushed him toward Beckett.

'Listen here, you little weasel,' his snarling voice boomed down the line, taking Mike by surprise. The line instantly went dead. 'Stupid fool, he hung up on me!' He angrily slammed the phone down. The calmness instantly dissolved. Jemison picked up the phone quickly and jabbed his finger down on the push buttons, 1-4-7-1 to retrieve the calling number from the automated operator. He listened with impatience. 'Fuck!' he screamed. 'The number is withheld.'

'If you had left Jonno on the phone, he may have got some answers for us,' Beckett said at his comrade's impetuosity.

'Don't go down that avenue with me,' he sharply reprimanded Beckett.

'I'm not here to argue with you. What happens now?'

Jemison composed himself, considering the next strategy to act upon. 'We'll take Jonno with us. He'll be the pawn in the next round of negotiations and Mike Harley will listen. He won't evade me a third time.' The men made their departure.

CHAPTER THREE

Mike Harley felt a shudder creep up his spine, and he quickly replaced the telephone receiver. The menacing voice of Jemison sent fear through him. How had they found Jonno? Then realisation struck him; the saved telephone message and his contacts book. How could he have been so stupid? He had unwittingly led the two men to his friend. He reached out for the receiver again, ready to redial Jonno's number.

Mike's mind swam with thoughts. Were they waiting for him to ring back? Was Jonno under instruction to locate him? He mulled over his options and decided to wait a while. He was grateful that he had taken the precaution of withholding the café's telephone number before dialling and that he had not disclosed his location to Jonno. It had been an automatic reflex on his part, practised many times before.

He wondered for a moment whether his hasty action to hang up when he heard Jemison's voice had jeopardised Jonno's safety. Were his other friends safe if the men had his contacts book? Should he call the police? He felt unable to make a decision about the best course of action.

'Are you okay over there?' Midnight called out to him.

'Yes, I'm fine.'

'You're acting a little strangely over that phone call.'

It surprised Mike that she had observed him. 'I had a crosswire on the line,' he said and smiled at her.

'Are you are sure about that?' She eyed him with some suspicion and Mike wondered if she had overheard the conversation.

'Something smells good,' Mike said, changing the topic.

'Grab a table and I'll bring breakfast over.' The cross-examination was over for now as Mike sat at the table where they had drunk their tea. Midnight came out from behind the counter; she carried two plates over and laid them down onto the table. She was to join him for breakfast. Mike looked at his plate of a full English breakfast, consisting of sausages, bacon, tomatoes, baked beans, fried bread and scrambled egg. The mouth-watering delight tempted him, and the aroma of cooked bacon overwhelmed his sense of smell. He was usually a cereal and juice man. They both picked up their knife and fork and started to tuck in.

Once breakfast was consumed and Midnight had returned to the kitchen, Mike felt that he needed some decent sleep; a clearer head would be of more use in making a sound decision about what he should do. He picked up the key from the table that Midnight had given him and headed for the door that Midnight had pointed out. She came out of the kitchen, carrying a tray of mugs and small plates to the counter.

'I'm going upstairs for some sleep,' Mike remarked to her and picked up his holdall, which sat by the door.

'I'll try and keep the noise down in here. It's top right.' She smiled.

He opened the door and left the café behind him. Mike started to walk up the bare wooden stairs, which creaked in places and were lit by the emerging light of dawn that peeked through the window at the top. The walls were drab, a faded buttercup colour, in need of a fresh lick of paint. He reached the landing and strolled to the door on the right, as instructed by Midnight.

Turning the key in the door and opening it, an overpowering musty smell assailed his nostrils. Pushing the door open wider, Mike could now see the room, bathed in faint light from the window. He walked in, tossed his holdall to the bare floor, as ripples of dust swirled in the air in their own little tango. A layer of dust coated the room's contents; the room was obviously rarely used.

Mike walked to the window. The catch covered in cobwebs and he cleared their formation and released the catch. He tried to heave the window up but it was tightly wedged and he fought to free it. Finally it nudged up. A chill breeze invaded the room; at least it eased the stale odour. Mike felt the cold bite him and checked the room for a source of warmth. There was no radiator in evidence and a cast iron fireplace stood bare. No available heat was to be seen.

He inspected the chest of drawers and wardrobe near to the door. The old brown timber was from an era when skilled craftsmen handmade furniture. How he wished he could use the wood to make a fire.

Mike's attention was drawn to the corner of the room nearest the window, which housed a sink unit. Orange rust stains cupped the rim of the plughole where water had stood an eternity ago. The mirror above it, with brass framework, hung from the wall supported by string and held by a nail. He turned on the hot water tap and the water flowed freely. It took a little while before it became warmer and it pleased Mike that he now had some form of warmth.

Mike walked over to the bed and slowly pulled back the bedspread. A cloud of dust particles was released. He removed the spread and laid it down gently onto a wooden chair next to the bed, keeping dust clouds to a minimum.

He looked to the opposite side of the bed, where a bedside cabinet stood. On its surface there was an old round-faced silver wind-up clock with a miniature hammer in between its two top bases.

The room wasn't modern by his standards, the walls were in need of redecoration, but it was a good temporary hiding place from his pursuers.

Early Memory

He went over to the curtains and tugged them closed. The room was a little fresher now. He was ready for some sleep.

The search of Jonathan Masterson's apartment enabled some startling discoveries for DCI Scroggins and DS Atkins after they secured a key from the landlord. The smashed lamp on the floor, an unmade bed in an immaculate home and the specks of blood found on the armchair and telephone gave them a new investigative angle.

It disturbed Scroggins. 'What're the odds on two merchant bankers from the same firm going missing?' He asked Atkins. 'There's more to this Roberts murder than we thought. It was a professional kill.'

'I agree, sir. It's possible that they may have been taken against their will. Harley's home was a forced entry and a struggle has taken place here.' Atkins offered his insight.

'Why? What's the motive?'

'Could be a banking deal gone wrong and someone wanted payback.'

Scroggins nodded in agreement with Atkins theory. 'As an alternative scenario, a fraudulent deal going wrong and perhaps Harley and Masterson fell out over it.'

'If the third party had criminal connections on such a deal.' The two were thinking along the same lines now.

'Could be an interesting case to pursue. If only we could get one of them, then we could put the pieces together, see what triggered it off.' Scroggins said, wanting something concrete to go on. His mobile phone started to ring, his thoughts now interrupted. He pulled the phone from his jacket pocket. 'Hello, DCI Scroggins,' he said, identifying himself to the caller.

'It's Mike Harley.' Scroggins was dumbfounded for a moment; he had wished for one of the missing men to appear and like a magician's trick to produce an ace, here was one of them. 'I just called my workplace and they gave me your number', Mike continued.

'Mike Harley, it's a pleasure to hear from you.' Atkins was surprised as he watched and listened to his superior with interest. 'My colleague and I are presently at your friend Mr Masterson's home.'

'Did you find Jonno?' Mike asked, hoping his friend was alive, perhaps traumatised by the ordeal.

'There's no trace of him. Why do you ask?'

'The guys who killed my neighbour were in Jonno's home earlier this morning when I rang. I hung up in panic when one of them came on the line.' A few jigsaw pieces were emerging for Scroggins to mull over.

'Do you know them?' He questioned, fishing for details to build up a case profile.

'I have never seen these guys before and it was Jonno who tipped me off about them. One of them is Jemison.' Mike added, remembering the name from the alleyway.

Scroggins was familiar with the name. 'Can you describe them?' The vital cog in the machinery of questioning. Mike gave the description. The name fitted the description and Scroggins knew that they were Jake Farrow's men. 'Where were you at the time of Mr Roberts's murder?'

'I was hiding at the far corner of the corridor and saw the bald-headed guy kill him.' Having a witness present at the murder scene was a good lead for them. He gave Atkins the thumbs up, indicating a positive outlook for the case.

'Who're they after and why?'

'It's me they want and I don't know why. Jonno probably knew, since he warned me.'

'How did Jonno warn you?'

'He left a message on my answer machine and I didn't clear it before I left.' There was a pause in Mike's speech as he relayed his stupidity. 'They probably heard it and took my contacts book next to it to find him.'

'There was nothing on it when we arrived at your place. Where are you?' This new evidence of Harley's plausible. Scroggins pulled out his notebook and pen. He wrote down the location. 'We'll send someone round to you but we will need to take a statement later. Your information is most useful. Thank you, Mr Harley.' He ended the call.

'Sounds like we have several leads to go on, sir.' Atkins intoned with enthusiasm.

'We need to get back to the station and I'll feed you the details on the way. Could you get the car ready while I give my wife a call and tell her I'll be working late?' Atkins nodded in agreement to the request and set off to leave Jonno's flat. Once he was out of sight, Scroggins dialled a number on his mobile.

'Jake Farrow, please,' he asked upon hearing the call answered. 'It's Peter Scroggins.' He waited several moments before Farrow came on the line. 'Why are you after Mike Harley? There's a man dead and one missing.' Both men started to talk and information was exchanged between them.

CHAPTER FOUR

Mike stood on the edge of the Old Market Square. A barricade stood in front of the arches of the square itself, making it inaccessible to any form of motor transport. Its steep cobbled pathway was preserved, and all four sides were Tudor-period buildings with their distinctive black beams, in a stand against the commercial architecture of modern buildings and roads.

The top-end houses, one of which was the *Midnight Oasis* café, were dwarfed by the towering presence of the church on the hill. The picturesque scenery took Mike's breath away. The walk around Old Beavonpool had helped him ease the nervousness of waiting for someone from the police to see him.

He walked across the quaint square to the café, which was bustling with customers. He ignored them and went up to his room. Mike had been in his room no more than a few minutes, when a knock sounded on the door. He felt immense relief that someone had finally arrived. He felt that safety was within his reach as he went over to the door. He opened the door; a young blonde-haired woman stood before him. Her presence spooked him.

'Hello, Mike, you didn't expect to see me again?'

'Amanda, isn't it?' Mike said, not quite sure of her name, but he remembered the face well.

'You've got a good memory there,' her words teased. 'Aren't you going to invite me in? I haven't come all this way to stand here.' It jerked him out of the shock of seeing her again.

'Sure, come on in. I just didn't expect you.' He stepped back from the door and Amanda entered the room.

'No, you were expecting the police, weren't you?'

Mike was thrown into confusion by her remark. 'What is this?'

'I'm the reason you went on the run from Jemison and Beckett.' Her admission astonished Mike. Amanda looked around the room. 'So, this is where the Heartbreak Kid winds up.' The sarcasm was chucked at him. She turned to face him, the door now closed. 'You have no idea who my father is and that ignorance has buried you in deep shit,' she said, not mincing her words.

'Are you telling me that our one night stand warrants the death of my neighbour?'

'No, *your* one night stand,' she corrected him brutally. 'He wasn't supposed to have interfered and you can never predict Jemison and Beckett's behaviour when provoked.'

'Oh, come on,' Mike said, refusing to accept total blame.

'Listen here, you prick, I never consented to being used just for a night.' A little anger escaped from her. 'How do you think I felt to wake up and find you gone, with your stupid calling card sitting there?' She reached into her coat pocket and pulled out a card. 'Another conquest for the Heartbreak Kid,' she read from the card and flung it into his face with fury. 'Are you so fucking insecure that you have to bed women to feel good about yourself?'

'I never saw it like that, you dozy cow.' The verbal attack inflamed Mike into returning the blitz against Amanda. 'It's a power game of sexual control.'

'A game that plays with people's lives, like your neighbour.'

The words startled Mike, and his anger rapidly disintegrated. The message hit home.

'Just who is your father?'

'Jake Farrow, one of the top lynchpins in the criminal network.' Amanda spoke calmly. Mike's mind gunned into meltdown at the revelation. Trust him to pick the daughter of a crime lord for a conquest! His mind dredged up the unwanted statistic.

'Can I put matters right?' He queried nervously.

'My father has a proposal for you to avoid further bloodshed.' Mike listened in anticipation to the absolution. 'He wants you to marry me.'

'Fuck off,' he turned down the proposal without any consideration. 'Just for a one night stand?'

Amanda unbuttoned her coat and pulled it back. Mike eyed the visible bump on her stomach. 'Yes, if you take your responsibility as a father.'

It horrified him. It was the first time a pregnancy from his conquests had tracked him down. He had always covered his tracks. 'How can you be sure it's mine?' he demanded. 'You weren't exactly squeaky clean yourself.'

'Are you discrediting me and trying to shame my father? Her annoyance bit deep. 'Maybe this will change your mind.' Her hand ploughed back into the coat pocket. Another item was brought out. Amanda handed it to him. Revulsion gripped Mike; his hand grasped his mouth as he looked at the photo. It was Jonno's face, bloodied from a clear bullet entry to his temple; his eyes were wide open in death.

'You didn't have to kill him.' Mike's voice trembled with sudden grief, his body contorted with shaking.

'Jemison had planned to exchange Jonno for you but once you rang the police, it changed everything. My father isn't keen on people who grass and your friend had to pay the price for his indiscretion.' She showed no emotion.

'You expect me to marry into your sick family after that? No chance.' He spoke with bitterness, and thrust the photo back at her.

Early Memory

'Sorry to hear that, Mike.' She turned towards the door. 'The next time I see you will probably be to dance on your grave.'

The chilling prediction left him cold for a moment. 'Get out,' he seethed. Amanda faced him at the door. She blew a farewell kiss in his direction, opened the door and left. Mike felt his stomach churn and he vomited.

Mike was sitting in a lonesome boat at sea, drifting aimlessly, with no oars to guide him. Waiting to be rescued from his peril, the storm clouds gathered momentum. The boat began to sway, waves were lashing against it. A roll of thunder sounded in the near distance, followed by bolts of lightning. The boat rocked ferociously, the waves rose higher, smashing against the boat, and water rapidly filled it. Mike his bared hands, frantically trying to bale it out. He was slowly drowning; there was no help in sight, his body wavered against the elements. A huge wave closed down on him, a killer, and was ready to wipe out his existence.

Mike woke with a sudden gasping for breath. Midnight leant over him. He realised that she had hastily shaken him from his nightmare, her hand now removed from his shoulder.

'Hey, are you okay? I haven't seen you for a few hours since your visitor left. It looks like you've been sick,' she said, eying the vomit on the floor.

'I was given some bad news about a good friend of mine who died. I think the grief made me sleep.'

'I'm sorry to hear that. Is there anything I can do to help?' She offered her support.

'No, I'm afraid I'm going to have to leave, what with the funeral to attend and all.'

The sleep had given him a clearer head to think about matters, even though he felt groggy. He knew that he had to get away into hiding once more after Amanda's statement that she would dance on his grave. In refusing marriage, he had signed his death warrant. With his hasty actions he had not thought through the consequences. Mike slid over to the edge of the bed and rose. Midnight stepped back from the bed.

'I'll leave you to it. My condolences once again.' She turned to leave the room. 'I'll see you downstairs for the keys, and there's no charge.' She left the room.

Mike started to pack his things. He quickly scooped up his belongings and randomly stuffed them into his holdall. The church on the hill attracted his attention as he looked out of the window. He somehow felt drawn to it, like a follower of the pied piper playing his bewitched tunes. He wasn't sure whether the good lord was beseeching him for a moment's prayer at his hour of need.

'Please, God, watch over me and save me from those who wish to harm me.' He surprised himself in his plea of a prayer. He had never been one for religion but felt compelled for some reason to act as he did. He snapped his mind away from the church, his thoughts refocusing on his escape. He picked up the holdall and went swiftly out of the room. He secured it and made his way down the stairs. He entered the café, and Midnight was at the counter. He went over to her with the keys.

'Thanks for your hospitality, it was much appreciated.' He handed the keys in.

'Going somewhere, Mike?' the voice of Jemison shot Mike's fears into overdrive. He turned sharply. Jemison and Beckett were sitting at a table. He eyed them in horror, his brow becoming moist. They gave him a twisted smile, gleeful that their prey was in the trap.

CHAPTER FIVE

The men must have travelled up with Amanda. Jemison rose from his chair.

'You'll be coming with us,' he instructed Mike. Midnight sensed that something was wrong from the fear showing on Mike's face. It certainly didn't seem like the two men were making a social call on him.

'I don't want any trouble here so I kindly ask you two gentlemen to leave.' Midnight raised her voice with authority. Mike stood still. The hub dub of conversation from the few customers in the café fell quiet.

'Hear that, Beckett?' Jemison faced his comrade. 'The lady wants us to leave after our custom.' Beckett rose to his feet. Jemison turned back to face Midnight. 'I don't particularly like taking orders from a woman.' The menace surfaced in his tone, his mood serious. He took a few steps towards the counter.

'Don't come any closer, sir,' she demanded, her hand swiftly sweeping under the counter and drawing a baseball bat.

The threat halted Jemison in his tracks. 'Whoa, steady on, lady, don't get your knickers in a twist.' He raised his hands in surrender and retreated a little. Midnight stood her ground. He retreated another step and turned towards Beckett. He slowly put his hands down, one moving towards the jacket's hip pocket. Mike saw the movement.

'Midnight, watch out.' Mike cried out.

The call came too late, as Jemison reacted more rapidly in his turn and now pointed a gun in Midnight's direction.

'You stupid bitch.' The defiance was spat out and people cowered at their tables. 'Did you really think that would scare me?' Jemison demonstrated with a little shake of his body, to mock her in her choice of weapon. 'I tell you what's scary—a freak like you with blue hair and lipstick.' Midnight remained silent at the insult.

Mike looked on in surprise that she still stood her ground, her face fearless at the sight of a gun in her face. It didn't escape Jemison's attention either.

'You want to be tough about this freak?' The gun slid across to the head of an elderly woman customer at a table. She started sobbing hysterically at the impact of the cold steel put to her head. 'I'll pop her if you don't drop it.' Midnight debated whether to call the man's bluff.

'I'd do as he says, Midnight.' Mike advised her. 'Two people are already dead because of them.'

'Including your friend who just died?' Midnight guessed. Mike nodded. She tossed the bat down, taking Mike's word.

Jemison withdrew the gun from the elderly woman's head and returned it to point at Midnight.

'A wise choice, and why defend a little weasel like him? It isn't your problem,' he lectured her on her interference.

'In a situation like this, I have a moral obligation to safeguard the welfare of my customers,' she firmly responded. Her stance brought guffaws from both Jemison and Beckett.

'Yeah right, you women never learn,' Beckett's wisdom was added to the conversation. Midnight kept a grip on her tongue, not eager to inflame the situation further. She stepped out from behind the counter, assessing the confrontation, watching the gun carefully. A wrong move would result in carnage.

'Get him prepped up.' Jemison ordered Beckett. The man went over and forced Mike's arms into a deadlock behind his back, his face forced down to a table. Beckett moved one of his hands into a pocket and pulled out a clenched fist. He moved it to Mike's mouth. Mike kept his mouth clamped shut.

'Open up.' Beckett demanded. He found no cooperation from Mike. He moved the fist away from Mike's mouth, brought it back to his side and swung it down with force onto Mike's back. Mike yelled in pain, and Beckett quickly jammed the tablets from his fist into Mike's mouth and clasped the jaw closed. Mike resisted attempts to make him swallow them. After another blow to his back, the pain soared again as he cried out. Cold coffee was poured into his mouth to help the tablets on their journey. The jaw was clamped shut again by Beckett's hands. Mike tried to keep up the battle as he fought against the pain and the contents in his mouth. He desired to breathe air and conceded, against his will. He swallowed them. Beckett released the lock on Mike's jaw. Mike gulped the air in desperation.

Jemison turned his head to Mike and chuckled at Mike's whimpering state. It was a bad move, as Midnight charged at him in a surprise attack. She caught him off guard, and grabbed Jemison's gun arm swiftly before he could react. She wrapped one hand tightly around his wrist, while the other pushed up his upper arm with force. A loud crack sounded.

'My fucking arm!' Jemison screamed out. He lost the grip on the gun and it fell to the floor. Beckett quickly threw a hand to his back and pulled a knife out, putting it to Mike's throat, to regain control. But Midnight had beaten him to the advantage. Her arms had Jemison's head in a lock and she was applying a little pressure to his neck. Jemison's only free arm frantically tried to relieve the pain, to no avail. Midnight had him secured, and now had the upper hand in the negotiations.

'You picked on the wrong freak,' she calmly spoke. 'I don't particularly like having a gun pushed in my face.' The grip tightened on Jemison's neck.

Beckett watched Jemison's sudden gurgle for air as a little life was squeezed out of him. It made him feel uneasy and he knew that they had just met a stronger foe. He withdrew the knife from Mike's throat and placed it on the table. He freed Mike. Beckett's surrender caused Midnight to loosen the grip a little on Jemison's neck.

'Mike, fetch the gun,' she politely ordered him. Mike picked up the gun and handed it to Midnight. She never took her eyes off Beckett in the process, unlike Jemison's error. It was a method taught to her in her earlier days of training, to make a move on an enemy when they had a lapse in concentration. A few seconds was all that was needed to make a difference between life and death. She had remembered well.

Jemison groaned more now, the pain from the broken elbow biting hard likes a scorpion's sting. He felt weak. Midnight brought the gun to Jemison's head.

'Want to play games?' she tormented him in a tit-for-tat move.

'No, please, I'll do anything. I just want the pain to stop,' his quivering voice begged. The menace had been ripped out of him.

'That I like to see—a man begging a woman for mercy.' She moved the gun away from his head and pressed it hard against the limp arm. Jemison screamed in agony with the extra searing pain. She was torturing him.

42

'The man needs a doctor,' Beckett shouted out, urging some compassion for Jemison. It pained him to see his buddy suffer.

'I know he does but I want him to learn a lesson,' she answered Beckett's plea coldly. She lowered her mouth towards Jemison's ear. 'You aren't such a tough guy after all, because I can eat guys like you for breakfast.' She then released him in Beckett's direction. The gun now focused on the two men.

Jemison tried to answer back to her taunt but was in too much pain as he held his damaged arm.

'Be a shame to carve up such a face,' Beckett threatened as the men retreated from the café. They left, and a few cheers erupted at Midnight's bravado, but she was in no mood to celebrate.

'There's nothing to cheer about,' she angrily scorned them. 'Somebody could have died. I want you all out, the café is now closed.' Nobody made a peep as they took to her request and got up to leave. 'No word to the police, either—I'll deal with it,' she demanded of them. She turned on Mike. 'You stay, because we need to talk.'

Mike could understand her annoyance at him. The violent drama was his fault. He had unwittingly drawn the men to interrupt this peaceful way of life. He couldn't, however, understand how a kind, hospitable woman could become such a fearless warrior in the face of adversity.   Whatever it was about Midnight, it scared him.

CHAPTER SIX

'What the bloody hell is going on?' Midnight demanded of Mike. 'There's also the matter of what they fed you, so I'll need to keep an eye on you for a few hours.' The anger was gone, replaced by concern for his welfare after the altercation.

It confused Mike that she could act so calmly over the whole episode. He was still shaken, more so by Midnight's conduct in breaking Jemison's elbow and the authority she had exerted over him. She was certainly no ordinary woman.

They were sitting at a table. Midnight had made herself a coffee but given just water to Mike. He started to tell her about the events. Midnight listened attentively. During their conversation, Mike started feeling uncomfortable. His eyes were fixed on the stairway door, alerted by a rumble. The door began bulging outwards, a pressure pushing against it. Midnight's words to him were drowned out into an echo as the force on the door became louder. A hinge started to jerk from its place, and water began trickling through the gaps. Did he leave a tap running after being sick earlier? He couldn't remember for sure.

'Shit, the place is getting flooded,' he interrupted Midnight.

She turned quickly. 'Where?'

'Can't you see it?' He pointed to the door in distress. 'It's going to go any minute.' The hinges were at breaking point as water poured more rapidly into the café. The door creaked, its defence crumbling. Midnight got up and walked towards it.

'Keep away.' Mike begged her. The door finally gave way; a torrent of water swept in and mowed down Midnight in its path and pushed the tables and chairs towards the other side of the wall. Mike felt his balance being thrown at the sheer volume of the deluge. He grabbed the nearest pillar to support himself as the room filled up.

Midnight opened the door. There was no trace of water; everything was as it should be. She turned back to allow Mike to see for himself that no danger existed. She was greeted by the sight of him with his arms clutched tightly around a pillar, his terrified face looking around.

'Mike, there's no flood. It's the drugs kicking off.' Midnight realised it was the effect of the tablets.

'Stay with me,' he called out, an arm reached for her. She knew her words were lost on him. She hurried over to help him and he grabbed her and pulled her close.

Movement by the door attracted his attention. Flames now sprouted from the surface of the water, reaching up and hugging the doorframe. An image developed before him as he watched, and heat drenched his brows.

'What do you see, Mike?' Midnight asked.

Early Memory

'A demon beckons us from the fire.' For once, he heard and made sense of her words. The demon loomed large. It had a red scaly body, the face of torturous lumps, horns emerging from the head, and nostrils flaring with fire when it snorted. It gave a snide smile as it looked primarily at Mike and then at Midnight.

'Vengeance is mine, Heartbreak Kid, when you are both hacked into tiny pieces of flesh for me to feed on.' The throaty whispers reverberated around them, followed by a piercing laugh.

'It's out to kill us,' Mike screamed out, his body shaking. Midnight had heard enough to diagnose the madness behind Mike's imagination.

'It looks like they've given you LSD and you're experiencing a bad trip.' She gently soothed him, careful not to worsen his fears. 'I want you to close your eyes, hold onto me and trust me to get us out of here.'

Mike looked quickly at the chaos around them, to search out an exit. 'I can't see an escape,' he blabbered incoherently.

Midnight put her hands to his face with a gentle firmness. 'It's important that you trust me, Mike. Remember what I did to Jemison without fear?'

Mike hesitated for a moment; the words swam around in his confusion. 'I trust you to save us,' he conceded, closing his eyes.

'Good, I'll guide us out to safety.' She began treading slowly, first to the counter, and switched

47

off all appliances. She picked up her coat and keys and then collected Mike's holdall before they went to the front door. She kept him at ease by talking every step of the way until they were finally out of the café.

'We are safe now.' The reassuring words allowed him to open his eyes slowly. The square was bathed in the late afternoon sun, people were milling about on their respective business. He attempted to look back to the café.

'Don't look back, leave your fears behind.' Midnight stopped him quickly. He obliged, nervously looking around him, his vision fuzzy. She had won his confidence and knew that she had to get him away quickly, before any more hallucinations disrupted that trust. She led him away. A lone figure on the corner of one of the square's alleyways snapped away at them with a camera. Out of sight to their unsuspecting eyes, its pictures would bestow darker days on them.

A summit meeting had been called at Jake Farrow's HQ. Jemison, Beckett and Scroggins awaited the man's arrival at his office. They were not allowed to talk, in accordance with the governor's rules that allowed him to conduct business on an equilateral level. The door swung open and Farrow strolled in with two henchmen alongside him. Farrow, in his trademark custom-made suit, full of his usual pomposity, walked over to his chair. One of the henchmen closed the door and stood guard by it, while the other walked with Farrow, who unbuttoned his jacket and sat down. The henchman stood next to him. Farrow rested his arms on the desk and clasped his hands together.

'I gave you simple instructions to bring Harley in but twice he evaded you when within your grasp.' Farrow said, his bombastic manner in full flow. 'Amuse me with your explanation on how a woman broke your elbow.' He eyeballed Jemison, whose arm was strapped up in plaster and in a sling. Jemison faced Farrow, a grey-haired man with the bushy moustache and short-cropped hair.

'She caught me off guard,' he responded nervously. 'The method she used to take control of the situation, it's like she was a high-level pro at some point,' he delivered his analysis.

'A pro, you say, yet you are supposed to be my best men.' Farrow showed his dissatisfaction and looked at Beckett. 'What level are we talking?'

'My guess is she had some kind of army training. She was fearless and even tortured him.' He sternly answered and pointed at Jemison, who hung his head in shame.

'It's not good if one of my best men gets tortured, is it?' Farrow asked sarcastically. The others agreed. 'If what you both say is true, why could someone like that be working in a café? It's not logical.' He rose from the chair and walked round to Jemison. 'Can I have your gun, please?'

Protocol stated that all weapons were handed in on arrival to Farrow's HQ. Jemison had broken the rules.

'The woman took it off me,' he declared.

'Give me one good fucking reason why I should not have you shot right now. You lose your gun to this so-called Superwoman and botch up a simple plan?' Farrow said angrily.

'Jake, don't be hasty,' Scroggins spoke out, the only man in the room allowed to call Farrow by his Christian name. All others used either 'Sir' or 'Boss'. They went back a long way. 'I have a solution to all this.'

'Fire away, you have my attention.' Farrow's anger was now disarmed. He had respect for Scroggins. He returned to his seat.

'If this woman is as good as your men state, we can fit her up for the murder of Roberts and Masterson. I would need her dead in order to pull it off.'

'An excellent idea, I like it,' Farrow exclaimed. 'Her prints are on Jemison's gun, so we just need a motive for the whole matter.'

'However,' Scroggins interrupted, 'Harley is of paramount importance. If he speaks to the police about my involvement in giving his location away to your guys while I sent my man on a wild goose chase, we are all in deep shit. I'll be damned if I have my police career in ruins when I'm so near to retirement.'

Farrow hushed him. 'I have always looked out for you, Pete, and won't allow that to happen,' Farrow promised him. He turned to face Jemison and Beckett. He held up a finger to them. 'I will give you both one final chance to redeem yourselves and sort this mess out.' The bombastic tone resurfaced. 'Harley shamed my daughter and refused marriage. I want him and the woman who defended him dead.'

CHAPTER SEVEN

A series of swaying motions woke Mike Harley. He was immediately confused by the surroundings and didn't know how he had got there. He looked around and saw that he was on a narrowboat. He seemed to be alone.

'Hello, anybody there?' He heard a male voice call out and several knocks on the boat's entrance. Mike stood up and it struck him that he wasn't his usual self. His balance was a little unsteady, his head felt like a hollow shell. Then a memory flashed back of the weird episode he had had. Mike remembered the tablets he was force fed and realised the experience wasn't real. The knocks continued persistently.

'Hold on a moment, I'm coming,' Mike shouted out to the caller. He composed himself and made his way to the entrance. He opened the door.

'Good morning to you, sir,' the chubby-faced stranger spoke. The hair was neat with a fringe; the overcoat was unbuttoned, revealing that the man was obviously a connoisseur of hearty meals and drink. 'Is Midnight home?' he enquired.

'No, she doesn't seem to be here,' Mike responded and he noticed that the boat was moored to a towpath next to a river. 'She may be working at the café.'

'It's all closed up and is usually open by now. I'm Greg Blunden.' He offered his hand for an introduction. Mike shook it but refrained from announcing himself.

'You must be the guy who got accosted by those thugs in the café yesterday,' Blunden said, getting straight to the point.

Mike became suspicious. 'How did you hear about that?' he queried.

'It's the talk of the town. What caused the commotion?'

The guy seemed friendly enough, Mike thought. He must have been a friend of Midnight visiting out of concern over the event. Maybe he was even a customer, considering his stomach.

'Oh, I just screwed around with the wrong woman and her father, Jake Farrow, is some kind of big shot in the criminal world. He sent his men out on me.' Mike summarised and felt at ease with Blunden.

'That's terrible. You ought to have gone to the police for protection.' Blunden's comforting words gave Mike cause to smile.

'That's the funny part—I did and instead of the police coming to see me, Farrow's men turned up with his daughter.' The statement took Blunden by surprise.

'I have friends in high places who can get this bent copper sorted out for you. Who is he?' Blunden offered his help.

'I can't recall the name but I've got it written down. Hold on a moment,' Mike said and rummaged in his trouser pockets. He pulled out a piece of paper. 'It's a DCI Peter Scroggins,' he read out and gave the paper to Blunden. He accepted it and stuffed it into his coat pocket.

'What I can't understand is, why didn't Midnight report the incident to the police?' he asked out of curiosity.

'That's because I had it all under control.' Midnight sternly replied, coming out of the woods by the towpath. Bags of groceries were in her hands. 'Who the hell are you?' she snarled at Blunden.

'Greg Blunden, the local paper's journalist,' he answered to Midnight. Mike stood horrified that he had given the man the story on a plate.

'I thought he was a friend of yours. He didn't say that he was a journalist,' Mike protested in his defence.

'You wanted a story on what happened at the café?' she angrily laid into Blunden. 'Nothing worth reporting on, I can tell you, so why not just clear off,' she demanded.

'According to witnesses, I'm told you had a gun in your face but you still came out on top. In a ruthless way, I might add,' he said.

'It was a storm in a teacup situation and people exaggerate what they see. I defended my customers with a baseball bat, so it's no big deal.' Midnight undermined Blunden's potential news story, the anger now replaced by diplomacy. 'Sorry that people misled you.'

'I don't buy that because there's more to you than meets the eye. Nobody knows where you came from. You just appeared from nowhere and nobody knows you personally. I think that you are hiding something,' he probed, watching Midnight's reaction carefully. Mike too showed interest.

'Your time is up, Mr Blunden, and you are wasting my precious time, so please leave.' Midnight replied, without so much as a blink of an eye.

'I guessed you wouldn't cooperate, but mark my words, I will find out who you are and get this story out,' Blunden promised as he passed Midnight on his way off the boat.

It triggered a reaction from her. She grabbed the collar of Blunden's coat and shirt and dragged him back for a moment. She faced him. 'You'll be playing a dangerous game if you print one word about this,' she menacingly told him, her hand grabbing his neck tightly. 'Bad people will want you dead when it comes to me, because I no longer exist. Save yourself by not being foolish.' She released him. A shocked Blunden hastily departed.

'That was a bit harsh, don't you think?' Mike said.

'You are in no position to judge me. Just remember that I saved your life from those lowlifes, so a little respect here, please,' she beseeched him and went inside. Mike followed.

'If you are trying to hide your past, why risk it by helping me yesterday?' Mike curiously asked. 'You could have let them take me.'

'No, I wouldn't. It's my instinct to help those in need from the bad guys, after what happened to my parents. Having that gun in my face just set me off,' she confided, giving a hint that she had fought against the likes of Jemison and Beckett before. 'How are you feeling this morning?'

'I feel a little light headed,' he answered, sensing that Midnight had switched to caring mode, avoiding further issues of her past.

'It looks like they doped you with LSD but breakfast will put a shine back in your step,' she smiled chirpily, the commotion with Blunden already a distant memory. 'If you want a shower, the bathroom is down on the left-hand side.' She pointed it out and started to unpack the groceries at the kitchen unit.

Mike walked towards the bathroom, picking up his holdall opposite where he had slept, with Midnight playing on his mind. Whatever had happened in her past, it had to be bad if she didn't exist anymore, in terms of identity. He wanted to know more about her and felt the utmost respect for her saving his life. It struck him that his moment of prayer had delivered him from harm. Midnight was his angel of mercy. He was grateful to be on the good side of her and, just maybe, he could become her friend in time. He went into the bathroom.

It seemed an eternity since Blunden had sat down at his desk at *The Beavonpool Mercury*. Deep in thought after Midnight's words, it haunted him to wonder what would happen if he exposed her. He couldn't fathom whether she was bluffing or not; his eyes stared hard at the photos he had taken of her and Mike when they left the café after the incident with Farrow's men. The more he focused on the pictures, the more gut instinct told him he was sitting on a massive coup nationally. Who was Midnight? He needed to know for sure. He reached for his coat and pulled out the piece of paper that he had been given. He knew it would be the catalyst in preparing a groundbreaking story. Blunden reached over to the telephone on his desk and dialled the number.

'DCI Scroggins,' came the reply after only a few rings.

'What would your superintendent say if I exposed you as a crooked cop?' Blunden threatened.

'Who is this?' he demanded, taken by surprise.

'Greg Blunden, a journalist. And why, instead of police protection, did you send out Jake Farrow's men to Mike?' he tormented, the game in play.

'Shit,' Scroggins muttered, not pleased that the press were now involved in the situation.

'It'll be a shame to have your police career in tatters with the story I intend to run, but we could cut a deal.' Blunden sensed the anxiety in Scroggins's voice and knew that he now held the ace in negotiations. He had the power to bring down Scroggins.

'What do you have in mind?' Scroggins conceded.

'I have photos of this Midnight woman, who fought Farrow's men and my witnesses of the incident says she was a lethal force. I suspect she has a hidden past and your police records may have something on her,' Blunden confidently said.

'You want me to ID her?' Scroggins replied with interest.

'Yes and if you can identify her and have something on her, I demand exclusive rights to a story on her and by return, will exclude any reference to your involvement with Farrow's men.' Blunden spoke, the adrenalin pumping away for the probable scoop.

'What if I can't ID her from the photos?' Scroggins urged, focusing on the finer aspects of the deal.

'I won't name you if there is evidence to support this but surely there must be something on her.'

'It sounds reasonable to me. Send me the photos by e-mail,' Scroggins said and gave out his e-mail address, safe in the knowledge that he could buy some time to save his career and possibly discover Midnight's identity in the process. 'Let's keep this matter between ourselves until I get back to you.'

Blunden agreed to the request. The two men finished their conversation, with a deal now set between them.

CHAPTER EIGHT

With breakfast now behind them, Mike Harley and Midnight had settled down to talk at the kitchen table. Midnight spoke first. 'You can stay with me for a few days to get the drugs fully out of your system but then you'll have to move on, as I can't guarantee your safety.'

'Surely Farrow's men won't come back?' Mike said. 'I could be anywhere by now.'

'Believe me, I know men like Jemison. They will want revenge—I hurt their precious pride. You heard Beckett say he wants to carve my face up.'

'The whole thing is my fault and it wouldn't be fair on you to put up with their threats. I should stay and face the consequences of my actions.' Mike said defiantly.

'Or you can swallow your pride and marry this Amanda.'

'No bloody way,' he scoffed; amazed that Midnight had even thought to say it.

'Well, it's a damned better sight than being dead.' She gave him the stark reminder of his choices. It brought the reality home to him.

'You certainly don't mince your words,' Mike said, a trifle annoyed at her attitude, which had made him see the obvious in the whole situation. It wasn't the scenario he wanted. 'How about giving me an alternative?'

'Are you any good with a gun?'

Early Memory

It took him by surprise. 'I have never used one in my life and wouldn't particularly want to,' Mike said uneasily. The prospect of taking up a firearm to defend his life horrified him.

'It's the difference between life and death, Mike. You can either continue to run and always look over your shoulder or you can stand your ground and force the issue to a conclusion. I won't think any little of you if you bottle it and run, because I can look after myself.' Her words rankled him.

'Are you saying I'm a bottler?'

'Yes, if you have got this far from Farrow's men,' she said, not hiding her views.

'Who the hell do you think you are?' Mike showed his anger at her statement. 'In my job as a merchant banker, I sometimes have to make instant decisions in a split second—whether to issue an instant loan to a long-standing company client of ours going under by the minute to help them stave off bankruptcy, or kill off their business altogether. That takes a whole lot of nerve to do that under immense pressure and I do my job very well.' He rammed home his philosophy loudly and clearly to Midnight's ears.

She smiled at him. 'The same kind of pressure that can be applied to saving your life from Farrow.'

It stopped Mike in his tracks, the anger evaporated. It got him thinking and he realised that she was right; there was logic behind it.

'Would you teach me to shoot if I stayed?' he asked.

'I take back what I said. You do have guts after all. Yes, I'll teach you.' She opened the drawer underneath the table and pulled out Jemison's gun and laid it on the table.

It shocked Mike for a moment to see the gun close up and he nervously picked it up. Midnight had given him confidence that with the right mind and strategies he could turn the tide of fear against the might of Jake Farrow. He surveyed the gun, now with a little eagerness.

The telephone buzzed internally on Scroggins's desk and he quickly picked it up. He gave his name.

'Sir, I found a match for the photo.'

Scroggins recognised the voice of the profiler he had entrusted with the search on the computerised database for clues to Midnight's true identity after receiving the e-mail from Blunden.

'I'll be right down.' He replaced the receiver and got up from his chair. It surprised him that a match had been found. Whoever Midnight was, for a record to be held she had sometime in the past crossed the law. He felt confident that it would be an easier job now, framing the woman for the murders of Roberts and Masterson. He soon reached the profiler and was pleased that his request for them to meet alone if a match were to be found had been carried out. 'What do you have for me?' he asked as he pulled a chair towards the profiler's workstation.

'One dangerous lady,' he replied and turned the visual display unit towards Scroggins.

He looked at the two photos of the woman and an unexpected result. Alongside the present-day photo issued to him by Blunden stood a younger photo of the woman, dressed in police uniform.

The profiler clicked on a box above the police photo. A wealth of information came up about the woman. 'She was one of us, with exceptionally high marks at police training college, especially in firearms, but she quit the force early on. Who would have thought of the career she took afterwards?' The profiler's tone was excited by the history they had on her. 'How did you find her?'

Scroggins read with amazement the mayhem the woman had caused. 'Why is the file closed?' He asked. It said *No Further Action*.

The profiler brought up another information menu on the screen. 'She's presumed dead, murdered by a gang who collected the bounty on her head,' he answered. 'You have proved that she is alive.'

'Keep this strictly between us, because we don't want to compromise her safety. I'll make a further discreet investigation into this matter. Can you make me a copy?' he asked of the profiler. The man nodded and got out a disk from his drawer and inserted it into the computer. As he waited for the disk copy, Scroggins realised the woman's identity brought complications. At least he now knew who the woman was and was ready to cast the net himself to catch her in a web of deceit.

CHAPTER NINE

Another section of branch shattered into scattered pieces from the velocity of a bullet slammed home with precision.

'Good, you're hitting them with regularity now.' Midnight spoke in admiration at Mike's progress in his firearms training. 'You're ready for Farrow's men.'

'Thanks to having a good teacher,' he complimented her. He brought the gun down from the target. 'Who taught you to shoot?'

'I did police training college, but it was an associate of my father who really nurtured my skills. He was an ex-military man and taught me well.'

'The police?' Mike exclaimed in surprise.

'Only for a short period of time,' she answered with a smile. 'I had more pressing issues to deal with.' She was careful in her choice of words, not revealing too much, but she had stirred Mike's curiosity. 'How do you find handling the gun?' She diverted the subject from her background.

'It's good. I feel a fighting chance of surviving against the odds.'

'I'm pleased for you, Mike. Let's get back to the boat before the gunshots arouse suspicion,' she said, urging caution, aware that they should not loiter too long in the woodlands. Mike nodded in agreement and they started the trek back.

Approaching the boat, they were surprised to see Greg Blunden standing there. He caught sight of them.

'Just the people that I wanted to see,' he said cheerily. 'Did you hear the gunshots?' He pointed to the woodlands, an indication that he had been there for some time.

'Yes, we heard them but it's only the farmer,' Midnight responded quickly. 'He's having trouble with poachers in the woods'.

'The farmer,' Blunden said, not convinced by the explanation. Midnight sensed this and opened her shopping bag.

'You should try his stuff,' she allowed Blunden to see the contents of her bag, which held farm produce of eggs, milk, cheese and some vegetables. Midnight had ensured that they had an alibi lined up, by visiting the farmer first before their shooting practice. Blunden seemed to buy the cover story. 'What brings you here?' she demanded.

'DCI Peter Scroggins wanted to speak with you,' Blunden answered and pulled out his mobile. He dialled the number and passed the phone to Midnight. She took it from him.

'Hello,' she said cagily.

'I want to propose a trade with you,' Scroggins said sternly. 'Give me Harley and I'll let you walk free with your true identity hidden. I know who you are.'

'You're bluffing.'

'I'm sure the journo would be happy to know about Marie Jessard.' The shock was etched on her face, and was noticeable to Harley and Blunden. After all these years, someone had spoken her real name. The past was no longer dead and buried.

'How can I be sure that you would keep your word?'

'I'm a policeman,' Scroggins replied.

'A bent one from what I know. To be associated with Farrow, I would need some form of assurance.' The men saw that Midnight wasn't comfortable with the discussion. Scroggins had rattled her cage.

'That's both of us in a catch 22 situation, then,' Scroggins cautiously said. He hadn't banked on Marie Jessard knowing of his link to Farrow. She sensed the uneasiness in his voice and recovered her composure.

'Cash wouldn't be out of the question, say 40 grand?' she struck her demand for assurance.

'Where am I supposed to find that?' he asked alarmingly.

'Speak to Farrow. I'm sure he'll help you out. I want the cash delivered up front with Blunden as the go-between before it can happen.' She chose her words with care. 'When it happens, I want Jake Farrow there with Jemison and Beckett. Nobody else. A no show by these guys and we can forget the whole thing.' She had the upper hand.

'I'll have to speak with Farrow and get back to you on that.'

'You do that,' and she immediately disconnected the call. She handed the mobile back to Blunden, pleased that she had forced Scroggins into a corner. 'Half that cash would be yours if I can buy your silence should DCI Scroggins disclose who I am.'

Blunden was at a loss for words. The cash offer was tempting but he wasn't happy that Scroggins had withheld her identity from him. He took his phone back.

'Scroggins has got you scared, hasn't he?' Mike asked.

'The stakes have changed. It's a matter of life and death now,' she coolly answered Mike. She turned and glared at Blunden. 'Be on your way and don't come back until there's an answer from Scroggins.' He took the hint and scurried away. Marie made her way to the boat. Mike chased after her and grabbed her.

'What is it?'

She waited for Blunden to be out of sight before she answered. 'There was a bounty out on my head and more ruthless criminal masterminds than Farrow had been led to believe that I was dead. It's been paid out. Imagine the complications if they find that I'm alive and well. I'll be worth more to Farrow now than you'll ever be.' She broke free of Mike's hold.

Early Memory

'You think Scroggins has told Farrow who you are?'

'I don't know, Mike. I'll have to weigh up the risks from all angles and if I'm going down, I want to take Farrow and his men too.'

'What about Blunden's story?

'I can't trust him. He made the contact with Scroggins and gave him something that helped to identify me,' Marie said sounding troubled.

'Being a journalist, maybe he sneakily got a photo of you and sent it down to Scroggins,' Mike offered a probable insight.

'Of course, picture profiling.' It made sense to her now how she could have been found out. 'Let's hope that money can buy Blunden's silence, but can I count on you for an ally?' she asked Mike.

'Of course you can. We'll go down fighting together,' Mike offered his support.

'Marie Jessard's the name, but it's only for your ears,' she introduced her true self and smiled. He couldn't believe that she had revealed her identity to him. In doing so, he felt that she trusted him. But Marie's smile hid another agenda; Mike would be scarified as the pawn in the trade off for her survival and the foundations were being laid.

CHAPTER TEN

'Forty thousand pounds?' Jake Farrow angrily exclaimed in his office. Another summit meeting on Mike Harley was in session. 'Why should I pay it to this Midnight woman, just to get Harley, and see my precious wad go away with her?'

'Trust me on this. You'll get your money back.' Scroggins coaxed. 'You do want me to nail her in a frame up and save your boys' necks on murder charges, don't you?' The ultimatum got Farrow to cut short his tirade.

'Why the cash, though? Surely we can pursue other avenues?' he questioned, now with diplomacy.

'She requested the cash as an assurance for the trade off. Failure to do so and it's possible that she may become Harley's alibi and put us all in the shit. Are you prepared to take that risk?' Scroggins championed his cause.

'Okay, you sold me on this, but I want my money back the same day,' Farrow demanded, stating the conditions of the deal. Scroggins agreed to the request. Jemison was wary of the whole thing.

'Can I say something, boss?' he interrupted the two men. Farrow gave Jemison permission to speak. 'We are talking of a dangerous lady here, who fought to save Harley from us, but it doesn't make sense that she's prepared to trade him in without a fight. Is Pete holding something back from us about her?'

Farrow digested Jemison's views for a moment and then looked at Scroggins for an answer.

'I do have some information on this Midnight woman but it's purely a police matter.' Scroggins spoke in self-defence.

'It didn't stop you from turning a blind eye on my activities, when I have supplied useful information to you in the past,' Farrow said, taking over the argument from Jemison. 'You wouldn't be where you are now if it wasn't for me.' It was a timely reminder to Scroggins that he owed him. Farrow had sensed the uneasiness in Pete's answer.

'I know that you saved my life when I was knifed in the line of duty and I would have died but for your intervention. I have repaid that debt time and time again. I even helped to put some of your sworn enemies away, so don't start giving me the third degree here.' Scroggins made his annoyance clear at Jake's willingness to make the issue personal.

'It's not like you to be so defensive on matters that have crossed our paths. You're not bailing out on me, are you?' Farrow spoke in alarm at Pete's angry outburst.

'We agreed never to push the boundaries on our own territories if it jeopardises each other's position of authority, even when we were best mates as kids,' Scroggins delivered home the promise made between them.

'Not at the expense of valuable information that you're withholding from me, Pete, and you sure as hell look as if you are desperate to hold something back from me.' Farrow wasn't buying Scroggins's patter.

'Oh, come on, Jake,' Pete attempted to swing the situation his way. It didn't cut the mustard with Farrow.

Jake Farrow rose from his chair and faced his long-standing friend. 'You are now released from my service, but I can't just let you walk out of the door, Pete—you know too much,' Farrow sadly said. The statement wasn't what Scroggins had expected to hear. It shocked him that Jake had taken the step to terminate their history together. Farrow's henchmen moved towards Pete.

'You can't kill me over this spat,' Pete spoke out in horror, the foundations crumbling away on their mutual respect for each other. Their friendship had been severely tested over the years but not in Scroggins's wildest dreams did he expect that this day would ever come. They had always resolved their differences amicably.

'Reconsider, Jake,' Pete begged him. 'We have gone through so much together.'

Farrow disregarded Scroggins's request for clemency and took to his seat again. Judgement had been served. Pete's arms were now held in a lock by the henchmen and they started to cart him away. He fought for his freedom but with little success. They got him to the door. 'Okay, I'll tell you,' he cried out in desperation for salvation.

'Hold up,' Farrow called out to his henchmen. They halted. 'Take your last opportunity wisely, Pete.'

'Her name is Marie Jessard,' Pete blurted out. 'She took out Max Bateman and some of his cronies at his Tippcross Hill fortress.' The revelation sent shockwaves through the room.

Jake remembered well the reaction it had caused in the criminal underworld. He rose to his feet. 'Wasn't she supposed to be dead and a bounty collected on her?' he enquired in surprise. Pete nodded.

'Jeez, and to think Jemison and me took on the legend,' Beckett mustered his voice to the exchange.

'She was the only person to have breached his security compound and got to him when even the police couldn't get close enough,' Jemison added his comment.

'It's a remarkable act for anyone to take on.' Farrow summed up. 'Imagine the ramifications the news would have in our network if it came out that she is alive. Would the collected bounty be revoked and given to the new informant? No wonder you wanted to keep it quiet, Pete.'

'I'm not doing it for the money,' he protested.

'How else am I supposed to interpret your intentions?' Jake snapped back. 'If the shit hits the fan over the trade off, your career would end up in tatters, so claiming the bounty would be your sweetener, wouldn't it? Where would that leave me?'

'Nowhere,' Jemison called out. A smirk appeared on his face as he looked at Scroggins, accompanied by a silent tut-tut towards him at his misdemeanour to double cross the boss. 'We should take control of the trade off ourselves,' he added.

'Quite right, Jemison. I can't trust Pete on this one,' Farrow bluntly said, much to Pete's dismay.

'I'm not out to deceive you, Jake, believe me.'

'Why try to hide it then? Does anyone else know about this?' Farrow demanded.

Scroggins knew he was outmanoeuvred on the issue and gave the information requested.

'Get him out of my sight,' Farrow ordered the henchmen upon conclusion of the details. There was no reprieve given. Pete fought once more for his life.

'It's your funeral, pal,' Jemison gleefully said, happy to see a copper in submission. He waved goodbye to the tormented man as Pete was ushered out, screaming for mercy.

CHAPTER ELEVEN

It was late at night on Christmas Eve. Light snow was falling outside the window, watched by little Marie Jessard all snug in her bed. She was listening out for the sound of Santa Claus and his reindeers. A light shone upon the window and in her excitement, she crept over, hoping for a glimpse of the great man with his bag of presents. She had no such luck, as she saw the light grow brighter and approach up the lane towards their house; she realised it was a car. The fields on either side of the lane glistened with whiteness, brightening up the night. The car pulled up outside the house. Its lights went out and a man emerged from the car and started to walk up to the entrance. Marie gently tiptoed over to her bedroom door and opened it. A knock sounded at the front door. She made her way to the edge of the stairs landing and peered down towards the door. Her father made his way to the door and opened it.

'Hello, Fingers, long time no see. Come on in,' her father greeted the man. She watched the man come into view and as he reached for his hat, she gasped in fear when she saw that he only had two fingers on his hand. He must have heard her because he looked up in her direction and the hallway light showed he had a scarred face.

'Noooo,' Marie screamed in fright as she woke up from her sleep. The bedroom door crashed

75

open and the passageway light to shine upon Mike, the gun in his hand.

'What's happening?' he asked in alarm, having expected an intruder.

'I had a nightmare,' she answered and he saw that she was shaking a little. Without any thought, he went over to her bedside and sat facing her, putting the gun down. She put her arms around him like a frightened child and held him close, her breath a little ragged. It surprised Mike that Marie could be so vulnerable. He put his arms around her too. After a short while, she pulled back a little from him, her head bowed, and Mike caught sight of her left breast exposed by the large loose T-shirt she wore. It aroused him. He leant in to kiss her. Her head lifted as she responded to the kiss he planted on her lips. She pulled herself towards him once more and a torrent of passion swept over them. Mike's hand slowly slid its way up her body until he caressed her breast. She trembled for a moment.

'Fuck me,' she whispered into his ear and he slowly tugged off her T-shirt, before lying her down and making love to her.

Marie sat in the kitchen area with a mug of coffee as the light of dawn streaked through the boat's window. She was angry with herself for letting her guard down and allowing Mike to take advantage of her vulnerability. She had lost control for the first time in ages, but what bothered her more was the return of her long-buried nightmare of the last time she had seen her parents. Her whole past had started to come alive again after Scroggins revealed her true identity. It spooked her and she knew she had to remedy the situation quickly for survival.

'Morning, gorgeous.' Mike's words startled her from her thoughts. She turned to him. He was in a cheerful mood. 'Any coffee for me?'

'Last night was a fucking mistake,' she scolded him, the smile wiped off his face.

'Come off it, we both wanted it.' Mike tried to lighten her mood with banter.

'What by trying to take advantage of a vulnerable woman? Only a bastard would have done that,' she spitefully laid into him. 'I take it I'm another Heartbreak Kid conquest to you?'

'Not at all, I thought there was an attraction between us. I'm sorry about that,' Mike quickly backed down, shocked by her reaction to their night. Her calm exterior in the face of a crisis dissolved before him.

'It won't be happening again,' she warned him.

'What's causing this change of mood?' Mike probed her. 'Is it the pressure of your identity coming out?'

'Not at all,' she sternly denied, not allowing her vulnerability to become the issue. 'I just don't like it when someone uses me for sex when I didn't have full control of my emotions.'

'Look, I said I was sorry.' Mike calmly spoke, trying to remedy the dispute between them. 'Let's be honest here. You did tell me to fuck you in the heat of the moment, so it's not all my fault, is it?' It struck a raw nerve with Marie because she knew that he was right.

'Okay, let's forget about it and put it down to a stupid mistake between the both of us, with no blame attached. Sorry for having a go at you.' She knew she had to back down quickly on her accusation and bit her anger because she needed Mike onside for the trade off to go smoothly without a hitch. She sipped from her mug.

'That's fine by me.' Mike was relieved that they had resolved the issue, and seeing Marie drink her coffee, he turned to the percolator on the kitchen's worktop and saw a clean mug ready for him and he poured his drink.

'After breakfast, could you do me a favour, Mike?' Marie kindly asked, getting their alliance back on track.

'Sure, fire away.'

'Can you get the groceries this morning, as there's a few things that I need to sort out?' Mike agreed to the request and Marie got up from her chair and started to prepare breakfast for them.

Mike rummaged throughout the kitchen and lounge area, picking at items, flummoxed in his search.   Marie had been observing him for a moment, before asking, 'What's up, Mike?'

'I can't find my mobile. Have you seen it?'

'No, I haven't. Why do you need it when you're only buying groceries from a farm?' she enquired suspiciously.

'I just want to make a few calls and make sure that nobody else has been killed like Jonno. Things have gone a little quiet for my liking. It's been two days since Scroggins rang you.' Mike showed his concern.

'The waiting game doesn't suit anyone. Leave it to me Mike and I'll chase it up, if Scroggins's silence is unnerving you. Remember, it's me that is more important to them now,' she said, hoping to allay his fears.

'Okay, you know best. I'll get the groceries.' Mike got ready to leave. 'Keep an eye out for my phone, will you?'

Marie nodded. She watched him leave the boat and walk off towards the woods. Once Mike was out of sight, she made her way to her bedroom and went over to a corner of the room. She lifted the carpet and bent down to loosen a panel of wood free from its resting place. She pulled out a small-concealed bag and opened it. Not for a long time had she felt the need to use the equipment at her disposal but she had already thought of Mike's concerns before he spoke them that morning. Scroggins's silence was unnerving. Marie took the bag to the dressing table, switched on the lamp that stood on it and took some of the contents out of the bag. She opened a drawer and took out Mike's mobile. She picked up a screwdriver and started to take off the back to the mobile, working toward her survival plans.

Mike was en route to the boat after getting the groceries, his mind in deep thought over the welfare of his friends, unaware that he was being tracked.

'She got you running errands now?' a voice startled him from behind, halting his footsteps. Fear crept up on him, the two days' silence now broken.

CHAPTER TWELVE

Mike nervously turned round to face Amanda, expecting Jemison and Beckett to be with her, but she was alone. He kept his guard up; they were bound to jump out from behind one of the trees to apprehend him.

Amanda could see his uneasiness at her presence as he searched out the trees around them. She gave out a small laugh.

'Relax, errand boy, I'm on my own.'

'How did you find me?' he demanded, after quickly dropping the groceries and pulling out the gun from his fleece pocket. He aimed it at her.

The smile disappeared from her face. 'The journalist guy told Peter Scroggins that Marie lived on a narrowboat, and in this place, that isn't going to be hard to find,' she said nervously in response.

'Shit,' Mike cried out. The net was closing in on them. More importantly, Amanda knew Marie's name. 'How did you find out about her identity?' He cocked the gun, primed for action.

Amanda knew the answer was of paramount importance and was scared that Mike would shoot her if she didn't cooperate. She was seeing another side to him, a man full of hatred towards her, who felt confident with the gun in his hands and was now calling the shots.

'Peter was forced to tell my father. His life depended on it. Please lower the gun,' she begged him, her hand moving to her stomach and resting on her growing bulge. She feared for the baby.

Mike duly obliged but her answer and action had enraged him. He stormed over to her and grasped her throat with one of his hands. 'It's a power game to you all to put a gun to a man's head for answers. It didn't help Jonno because your father still had him killed when he revealed information. Where's the justice in that?' Mike spoke vehemently. He pushed the gun to Amanda's bulge. 'Let's settle this right now and do away with the problem.'

'No, please, not the baby,' she screamed out in horror, visibly shaken up by the whole ordeal. She burst into tears and started sobbing.

It was enough to shock Mike out of his violence. He released her from his grip. How had he become such a cold-hearted monster with the power of a gun in his hand? It changed his outlook, as if it had a hold over him, and he felt disgusted with himself.

'I can't believe what I just did. Do forgive me?'

'No, I'm the one that needs forgiveness,' Amanda stuttered among her tears. 'I've always wanted a baby and to have a special man in my life, but men get scared off by a powerful man like my father. I thought maybe if I got myself pregnant, he would disown me and banish me from the family so that I could find that happiness, but it's made matters worse, with him being more overprotective and vowing to keep the family name untarnished.'

'It's not an easy choice to make when you've a father like yours.' Mike was now feeling calm, and was unable to believe that he was offering support to an enemy that wanted to snuff his life out, but her words struck a chord with him. It reminded him that underneath the trials of life, we're all human, making the best of what fate gives to us.

'I thought I was comfortable living in a criminal family but this baby is making me realise that I don't want it to grow up in an atmosphere of fear or reprisals against my father. I'm sorry for dragging you into this mess. I came here to tell you that.'

'Is the baby really mine?'

'Yes, I'm pretty sure.'

'I'm prepared to take my responsibility and stand by you, but I will have to convince your father to hand Jemison and Beckett over to the police for the murders of my neighbour and Jonno. It isn't fair that I should compromise Marie's safety too.'

The statement took her by surprise.

'Do you really mean that? Why the change of heart after what I've put you through?'

'Getting the bloodshed to stop and re-evaluating my life, I guess.'

'I'll have to get back to my father quickly and be honest with him over my actions and stop you from being traded off dead.'

'What are you talking about?' The implications

hit home hard.

'Tell me that you knew that Marie was going to deliver you to my father to keep her past life hidden?'

The revelation shocked him. 'No, I didn't know.'

'Christ, she's more shrewd in her cunning than I thought. Believe me, Mike, she's not to be trusted. When a powerful man like my father is wary of her, it's saying something.'

Mike thanked her for the warning and the issues that they had raised for a solution to the whole problem. Amanda's words about Marie made him realise that there wasn't a solution, and deceit came with a heavy price: his life. He knew that he now had to challenge Marie for the truth and it was not something that he was looking forward to, as he quickened his steps to the boat.

Early Memory

CHAPTER THIRTEEN

The moment he got back on board the boat, he called out Marie's name loudly. It was several moments before she emerged from her bedroom.

'What on earth is this commotion?' she questioned, not pleased with his conduct. 'Waking up the dead by shouting out my name when we're supposed to be lying low? Have you gone mad?'

'No, not mad at all, but there's a reason, isn't there?' He eyed her with a steely look. 'Trading my life with Farrow to protect your past, wasn't it?'

'What happened? Have you spoken to Scroggins?' she demanded of him, her carefully laid plans in danger of being blasted to smithereens by a 'grass'.

'Dead men can't talk, can they?' he taunted, not making full sense of the answers she sought. It was an elaborative ploy on his part. 'Unless, they're got to before their grisly end.'

'Scroggins confessed to Farrow before he was silenced? Farrow knows who I am?'

'You got it in one.' Mike sarcastically applauded her. 'You wanted to give my life away to Farrow. How safe is yours now?'

'How did you know?' The foundations were crumbling fast on her survival and she wasn't comfortable. She had given her admission away.

'It was Amanda who told me. She knew you by your true name. Thanks very much for your so-

85

called trust between us.' Mike's words darted at her like lethal spears.

'You've every right to be upset over my deceit, but believe me—I did have your best interests at heart.'

'My best interests.' He fiercely slammed her words down and scoffed at the woman's nerve. 'This is my life we're talking about here.'

'You've got to realise, Mike, I stand to lose more than you ever will, so I need to cover my past.'

'Whose fault is it, to have a bounty hanging over their head?'

'Certainly not mine,' she coolly replied.

This riled Mike up. He couldn't believe that Marie was shifting the blame from herself. 'Just what is so special about your past that you have to hide from it and play dead?' He kept up the barrage. He wanted to get to the truth now.

'I took out one of the country's top crime lords and some of his men.'

'There's the difference between us, Marie.' He jabbed a finger towards her face. 'I've never killed anyone in my life, so if a life is to be spared, it should be mine, you selfish cow. You deserve to be hunted down and shot for what you did'.

'Not when the man had my parents murdered,' she bitterly screamed at him, her emotions forcefully bursting open at Mike's putdown.

'What?' The answer stung his anger. He had lashed out once again with no thoughts of what he was saying, leaving a destructive trail in his wake. Mike saw that Marie was upset, with tears welling up in her eyes, but she was bravely holding them back. He quickly apologised for his comments.

'When I realised that my parents didn't die in a car accident but were murdered, revenge was all I could think about. You do understand now, don't you?' Her voice was breaking with emotion.

'Yes, I understand, but why?'

'My father was once in Max Bateman's circle, known as the forger and responsible for cash heists, but once I was born, he wanted out for good. But Max wasn't going to let him go easily and tried to frame him a few times to keep him when he wouldn't reconsider his decision, but my father was astute and kept ahead of Bateman. He transferred a large sum of money into a secret offshore account for assurance, but his luck ran out in the end. My parents were taken from me one Christmas Eve when I was a small girl. That night haunts me in my dreams because I saw one of Bateman's men at our house. Wait there a moment.' Marie went off to her bedroom and returned with a large folder that she placed before Mike.

He opened it and was looking at newspaper cuttings. The first one he held and read related to a car accident with Marie's parents, where it was assumed that the car had skidded on black ice and gone over into the ravine. He then read the reports of the bloodbath at Max Bateman's hillside fortress, where an unknown female assailant had assassinated the man. Others had died with him. Further cuttings showed reports of a police search for Marie in association with the Bateman murder. A picture showed her in a police uniform. Finally, there were cuttings of her reported death in an isolated farmhouse, blown apart by a gas explosion after a shoot out against criminal gangs who were securing a bounty on her life. It was a lot for Mike to take in. He understood Marie a lot more clearly now. He looked up from the cuttings to face her.

'There are no secrets between us now,' she softly told him, her composure regained. 'My motive for the trade off is clear but it's now pointless, since Farrow knows about me and he'll probably opt for a new bounty on my life. He'll want us both dead, so we shouldn't be fighting each other. I'm sorry for what I was doing.' She was sincere in her words.

'How did you find out your parents were murdered and how did you get into Bateman's fortress?' he asked with curiosity.

'I went down to the wreckage some years later with an associate of my father's, who'll remain nameless, and found bullet marks in one of the tyres and became a girlfriend to one of Bateman's men and got access eventually.' She gave a warm smile to Mike, in confiding the answers to the ultimate questions. She trusted him freely.

Mike knew he had to do the same if they were to survive the wrath of Jake Farrow.

'I managed to hold an amicable conversation with Amanda earlier and there could be a solution soon because I've offered to stand by her and the baby. She's trying to get her father to halt the trade off.'

The smile dropped from Marie's face.

'Who's the deceitful one now?' she lambasted him. 'Save yourself and leave me in the shit. I saved your life at the café and remember, you got me into this mess. You owe me big time and we'll finish this together.'

'I know and we'll do so, too,' he assured her. 'I think we'll need to have tactics, because Amanda did say that Farrow was wary of you and he may try—' his voice stopped abruptly as footsteps were heard outside, boarding the boat.

Mike instantly pulled his gun out, while Marie picked up a sturdy knife from the kitchen counter. With their weapons aimed at the door, their breaths a little shallower, they were ready for the battle of survival.

CHAPTER FOURTEEN

'Hello, anybody home?' Greg Blunden called out as he landed a few knocks upon the door. The door flung open and they quickly pulled him in, their eyes fixed on the pathway as they did so.

'Anybody follow you?' Marie asked as Mike closed the door and bolted it.

Blunden felt alarmed, seeing the knife in her hand and the gun in Mike's hand. 'Not that I know, what's going on?' he nervously queried, his forehead starting to sweat profusely.

'We thought Farrow's men were on the attack when you boarded,' Mike answered. They disarmed their weapons.

'You're both right to exercise caution. I came to tell you that Jake Farrow has taken over the trade off because he rang me a short while ago and I think he killed DCI Scroggins. I've not been able to contact him at all.' Blunden wasn't speaking confidently now, he was clearly afraid of how events were unfolding.

'What did he say?' Marie cajoled him for further information.

'The trade off is set for dawn tomorrow at Frosike's Point. Farrow demanded that I'd be the go between to the two parties. I'm shitting my pants over this. I wished I had never rung DCI Scroggins in the first place when you warned me that bad men would kill me if I found out who you were. I have and it's happening, isn't it?' he blabbered, fearful for his life.

'Who am I?' she politely asked him.

'I can't tell you with Mike around,' Blunden said, remembering the need for secrecy.

'It's okay, he knows.'

'Jake Farrow said it was Marie Jessard. He assumed I already knew when he took over from DCI Scroggins and I checked you out on the archives. I can assure you, I have no intention of running a story on you. It's too risky and I value my life.' The man's change of heart surprised Mike and Marie that he would let go of a major scoop.

'Depending on the outcome of the trade off, there's always the piece about DCI Scroggins being a bent copper, you know,' Mike encouraged Blunden. It met with Marie's approval as she nodded in agreement.

The hint lifted Blunden's spirits a little.

'Whatever are we going to do tomorrow?' With more pressing matters on his mind and a handkerchief now in hand, he dabbed the sweat from his forehead.

'We need to be on our guard from now until dawn in case Farrow plans an early assault,' Marie told the two men.

'You may need this.' Blunden smiled weakly and pulled out a photo from his inside coat pocket and passed it to Marie. 'I downloaded Farrow's photo off the Internet, as he's the only one you both have not faced yet.' He had delivered the ace that had been overlooked for the trade off.

It meant a lot to Marie that Blunden was trying to make amends for his mistake of involving Scroggins. She leant over his portly frame and planted a kiss on his cheek. He blushed at the gesture, much to Mike's amusement.

'You're off the hook, now you've chosen the right side. I'll try to keep you safe too. Do you want to stay here for safety?' Marie asked.

'If it's no problem.'

'Not at all, let's sit down and plan how we are going to tackle the trade off in case Farrow brings in extra men.' The two men duly obliged in following Marie's request. The clock was counting down time to the confrontation, which drew ever nearer to them.

CHAPTER FIFTEEN

The day had arrived, and the dawn was ready to cast its light on a brand new day. Marie, Mike and Greg were in position for the exchange, having taken the decision to camp out in the wild for the night. It could have been their last night of freedom but it had passed without any incidents. The first streak of light pierced the darkness as a hazy redness glow. The sun was breaking through. Slowly, the hills and woods around Frosike's Point could be seen, the early-morning mist gently lifted after a cold night, as dawn brightened the sky. In the near distance, the shine of car headlights could be seen travelling towards them on a dirt road. Greg Blunden began his descent down on one of the hills from the giant rock that had been their hidden post and made his way to the meeting point. Soon the car was upon them and it stopped a little short of the gateway that stood before them. The lights went out and the engine was turned off. Doors opened and through binoculars Marie made out the figures of the expected men. Jemison, Beckett and Farrow himself with the duffel bag, as per the agreed conditions. She pulled the radio link to her mouth and looked in the direction of Blunden.

'Looking positive, proceed.'

'Will do,' he replied nervously via his link and walked to the gateway. Beckett stopped him and searched him, checking out his ID. Marie saw Beckett give his boss the all clear, that Blunden was unarmed.

Farrow walked up to him. 'Where're the others?'

'Right here, Farrow, where we can safely observe the exchange,' Marie responded via the radio link. She heard him clearly without any problems.

'Impressive link up, Marie, but before we can do business, I need to clarify that you're indeed here with young Harley and that it's not a ruse.' Beckett and Jemison were scanning the scenery around them, watching their boss's back for any attempted attack as he began the exchange.

Marie pushed Mike forward to stand in view for a moment. He did so.

'Is that Harley?' Farrow pointed him out to Jemison.

'That's him, alright.' Sighting confirmed. Mike ducked behind the rock once more, out of sight. Marie showed herself and Jemison confirmed her identity once more to Farrow before she hid again.

Farrow threw down the duffel bag to Blunden. 'The money's all there. Check it?'

'Check it out for any devices,' Marie advised Greg. He started to check out the bag. She watched from their post.

It amused Farrow.

'Marie, I've nothing to hide. I'm a respectable

businessman. I'm keeping to Scroggins's promise of keeping your life quiet in exchange for young Harley. You need not fear me. In fact, I've admiration for your job on Max Bateman. Pure class.' He chuckled in earnest.

'Save the bullshit, it doesn't work on me. How're we doing, Greg?' Time was precious and she wanted matters concluded quickly.

'Everything seems okay. It looks like forty grand is in here and there are no devices that I can see.' Blunden's words wavered, as he tried to remain calm.

'Prepare for exchange.'

Mike grabbed the radio from Marie. 'Farrow, have you spoken to Amanda?' He needed to be sure of her promise to him before he walked over to them.

'Yes, she told me that you offered to stand by her and take full responsibility for your actions. Did you mean it or were you just trying to save your life?'

'I meant every word because people have died needlessly.'

'Then you've nothing to fear, Harley, and I'll welcome you to my family.' He held out his arms. 'Don't keep your future father-in-law waiting,' he called out.

Mike was satisfied with the response. Amanda had sought the solution. As he prepared to move into view, Marie stopped him. 'Good luck, Mike, and watch yourself. Remember—trust your own self above anyone else.' She gave him that warm smile.

'Thanks for your help.' They hugged for a farewell and Mike was on his way.

'Exchange underway.' Marie radioed Blunden and he started to walk away from the gateway with the duffel bag. She switched to her binoculars and watched carefully. Things were too smooth for her liking but she had played it safe. Mike was now the open target. As Mike and Greg were about to pass each other, she halted them on the radio and the two men faced each other.

Blunden fished his hand into his coat pocket and pulled out Mike's mobile.

'Sorry I didn't give you your mobile back earlier, but Marie asked me to safe keep it last night. She wants the link kept open until the car is out of sight for your own safety.'

The phone rang and Mike answered it.

'Keep the line open until the exchange is over. I'm on Blunden's mobile,' Marie's voice greeted him. 'Proceed.' The two men shook hands and continued their walk in opposite directions.

Mike had almost been delivered into the hands of Farrow when a shrill gunshot punctured the calmness.

CHAPTER SIXTEEN

Farrow was down. Jemison rushed to his aid while Beckett grabbed Mike and pushed a gun to his head, retreating towards the car with speed.

'What the hell?' Marie spoke in bewilderment at the turn in events. She had expected someone to try and silence Mike and herself, but not Farrow—or was it a set up? Blunden scarpered past her, scared witless, and headed into the woods, clutching onto the bag for dear life. She looked through the binoculars and Jemison had now left Farrow alone. The man was dead. Jemison ran for the car and it hastily sped off as he got in. She could hear argumentative voices on the phone and put it to her ear. 'Mike, what's happening?'

'You double-crossing bitch,' Jemison screamed out at her down the line. 'I'll kill you for this.'

'It wasn't us,' Mike protested in the background but Jemison wasn't buying it.

Marie knew that she had to act quickly before the car got out of range. She pulled out the metal box from her pocket, flipped it open and turned the switch on. It hummed; the line to Mike's mobile was still open. She pressed the detonator and the car exploded before her eyes. She felt immediate satisfaction at the accomplishment of her mission to silence those who threatened to uncover her past.

'Oh God, no.' A piercing scream alerted her to a nearside section of the woods. Amanda ran out, armed with a rifle, her eyes fixed on the burning car.

It shocked Marie that Farrow's daughter had pulled the trigger. She dropped the detonator to the floor of their post to avoid detection and called out to Amanda. The woman looked toward her and Marie signalled to Jake Farrow's body as she started her walk toward it. Amanda did the same. The women came face to face over the body.

'I had to kill him because yesterday I finally realised that he was more interested in being a crime lord than he was in his own family's welfare. My happiness meant nothing to him, even when I begged him to spare Mike's life and allow us to be a family. He even talked of the baby as being an heir to the business. It's not what I want for its future.' Amanda spoke with bitterness and showed no remorse for her actions. She spat at her father's body.

'Your father's reign is over. Maybe now you can find that happiness with the baby when it's born and be in a family of love. I never got that chance when Max Bateman murdered my parents, so grab it freely,' Marie encouraged her.

'But Mike not here to share it, is he?' She shed a few tears for him. 'Life goes on, doesn't it?' She looked once more at the blazing inferno.

'Believe me, the pain will ease. You better get out of here before the police come crawling around.'

This stirred a reaction in Amanda and she broke off from her stance and lowered the rifle. 'I had imagined you to be a really callous bitch with the things you've done, but you're no different from me, except with more compassion, to have saved Mike from Jemison and Beckett's clutches at the café. I never did like them.' She allowed herself a small laugh at their demise. 'Thanks for listening.' Amanda started to walk away and Marie knew she had a small matter to attend to before she, too, could flee the scene. She walked back towards the rock that had hidden them for the trade off.

Marie arrived back at the boat after covering her tracks at Frosike's Point and sensed that something wasn't right. The door was slightly ajar, its padlock lying on the deck. It had been secured when they had left the boat. She felt the battle for survival wasn't over yet and that Farrow had sent some men there. If he had, would Amanda have known? She took a few cautious steps towards the door and smelt petrol wafting strongly from below. It immediately got her guard up that someone was attempting an arson attack.

'Is the phoenix ready to fall back into the ashes?' A gruff voice greeted her. The sound of a match being struck alarmed her and she turned to face her tormentor. As the man lit his cigar, the flame showed his scarred face and the hand with missing fingers. He blew out the match and smiled wickedly. 'Be a shame to burn you so soon, wouldn't it?' he sneered at her. 'How long has it been since our last encounter?'

'You know me, Fingers—I don't exactly hold you dear after you carried out the murder of my parents on Bateman's orders.' She showed him that she wasn't afraid. 'You were supposed to be a friend to my father.'

'It wasn't personal, purely a business matter. I know you were watching from the top of the stairs that night of my arrival. I wasn't exactly Santa Claus, was I?'

'What brings you here? Jake Farrow, by any chance?'

'Yes, he wants his money back and staked a claim for the old bounty. Did you really think he was going to let you walk free?' He puffed on his cigar in between words.

'You needn't bother to pay him, as he's dead.'

'Still a sharp assassin, I see.'

'I didn't kill him. His daughter did.'

'That's a surprise to hear. You know, people found it hard to believe when Farrow stated that you were alive and well. It's been entrusted to me, out of what's left of Bateman's mob, to verify your existence and to exact your death, considering we have so much history with your father.' He spoke in a honourable manner about the importance of her re-emergence.

'You mean a perverted desire to kill the

remaining Jessard to complete your collection? What about Bateman's money that my father siphoned?' she challenged him.

'It was never traced. Why do you ask?

'My father did leave me a legacy, you know. A book of contacts, evidence that will shatter the peaceful deal between some crime lords and bring warfare to the forefront. And the money—I've got it.' She smiled warmly at Fingers.

'You're bluffing.'

'Kill me and find out the hard way that blood will be on your hands, or I can pay you a nice sum to keep me free.'

Fingers knew it was a tough dilemma to call. He pulled the cigar from his mouth.

'They say that smoking isn't good for you. Shall we test the theory?' He threw the cigar at the boat and Marie tried to stop it but failed. It ignited.

Whoosh, the flames rapidly spread across the petrol trail, the boat now on fire. Fingers gave a maniacal laugh as he held a gun aimed at Marie. There was no escape for her. She felt the heat around her.

'Your old man tried similar tricks but it couldn't keep him alive. You don't fool me.'

'Police!' a loudhailer suddenly wailed. 'Put the gun down.' Fingers turned to see uniformed officers bearing down on him, some with guns pointed at him. He turned back to Marie, who leapt out at him from the flames, her face full of hatred. They wrestled on the ground for control of the gun. Marie, being much younger than Fingers, who was in his twilight years, was more than a match for him. She grabbed the gun and pushed it to the palm of his good hand. She squeezed the trigger hard.

Fingers screamed like a banshee, holding his bloodied hand. Marie moved the gun to his head.

'This is for my parents.'

'Don't do it, Marie. It's over. He's going to prison. Save yourself,' a plain-clothes officer called out to her. She relented and released him to a police officer that had just reached the struggling pair. She picked herself up and looked at her blazing home. Her time here was finished.

'You can run but you can't hide, Marie.' Fingers said, launching into a tirade. 'We'll hunt you down and slit you like a fish,' he threatened, before being bundled away from her sight.

'CSM Atkins.' The man that had called out to her presented himself, his ID card showing. 'I'm an associate of DCI Peter Scroggins and he's now in custody, for your information.'

'I thought—' she began.

'He was dead?' the officer interrupted. 'No, he's alive and well. Mr Blunden tipped us off to the events that had taken place and we found the DCI locked up in luxury at Farrow's home. He confessed to his actions. We tried to get here as quickly as possible but we were too late to save

Mike Harley. I'm informed that you became friends.'

'Yes we did.'

'I'm sorry, madam.'

'What happens now to me?' she asked of her fate.

'You can come with us and be put under police protection, go under witness protection or be free to go.'

'Free to go?' The last option surprised her. 'What about the Bateman case?'

'Not enough evidence to implicate you, as Bateman's mob made it an internal inquiry without the police being involved and even though your name was given, we'll have to take it as hearsay. The bounty didn't help their cause for a conviction. My view—you should be given a medal for your actions. You did us proud. Think it over, Marie, while I attend to this.'

She thanked him and he left her side.

Greg Blunden hurried over to her from the police cordon when Atkins had finished speaking with her.

'It was Farrow's daughter who fired that shot at the trade off. She's just been arrested and they found a detonator on Jake Farrow's body. He took Mike's life after all. What a waste,' he said sombrely.

'It is, but we survived Farrow.' Her words were hollow, as deep down, she felt Mike could have been allowed to live had she known that Farrow had lit the fuse to her existence in the criminal underworld. She could no longer have her past buried deeply. New strategies were needed for a new fight. Beavonpool was no longer her safe haven; her home was gone as she watched it burned. If it hadn't for the police, it could have been her funeral pyre.

She turned to Blunden. 'Keep the money. It's yours for getting the police here in time and saving my life. I'll have to get away from here.'

'Where will you go?'

'The less you know, the safer you and I will be,' she reminded him. 'Enjoy the scoop.' She held out her hand to him.

He shook it.

'Goodbye, Midnight, and be safe always.'

She smiled at his discreet reburial of her past. She left the scene behind her, with the early memory now avenged.

ABOUT THE AUTHOR

Mark is a deaf writer born in 1964, who has been living on the south coast of England for over 30 years. After many dormant years his writing dream was revived when in mid 1998 ill health caused him to lose his job on medical grounds. It was diagnosed as Menieres. During the recovery period, he enrolled in two creative writing courses that led to writing qualifications and two novels were written in that time, one of which was 'Early Memory', his debut publication release. A full biography of the author can be found at his Web site www.markradford.co.uk. He is presently working on his next novel.

ISBN 141205587-3

9 781412 055871